This book belongs to

..................................................

I celebrated World Book Day 2019
with this brilliant gift from my local
Bookseller and Puffin Books.

## CELEBRATE STORIES. LOVE READING.

This book has been specially written and published to celebrate **World Book Day**. We are a charity who offers every child and young person the opportunity to read and love books by giving you the chance to have a book of your own. To find out more, and for oodles of fun activities and reading recommendations to continue your reading journey, visit **worldbookday.com**

World Book Day in the UK and Ireland is made possible by generous sponsorship from National Book Tokens, participating publishers, booksellers, authors and illustrators. The £1* book tokens are a gift from your local bookseller.

*World Book Day works in partnership with a number of charities, all of whom are working to encourage a love of reading for pleasure.*

**The National Literacy Trust** is an independent charity that encourages children and young people to enjoy reading. Just 10 minutes of reading every day can make a big difference to how well you do at school and to how successful you could be in life. **literacytrust.org.uk**

**The Reading Agency** inspires people of all ages and backgrounds to read for pleasure and empowerment. They run the Summer Reading Challenge in partnership with libraries; they also support reading groups in schools and libraries all year round. Find out more and join your local library. **summerreadingchallenge.org.uk**

*World Book Day also facilitates fundraising for:*

**Book Aid International**, an international book donation and library development charity. Every year, they provide one million books to libraries and schools in communities where children would otherwise have little or no opportunity to read. **bookaid.org**

**Read for Good**, who motivate children in schools to read for fun through its sponsored read, which thousands of schools run on World Book Day and throughout the year. The money raised provides new books and resident storytellers in all the children's hospitals in the UK. **readforgood.org**

* €1.50 in Ireland

Jeff Kinney

by Greg Heffley's Best Friend

PUFFIN

PUFFIN BOOKS

UK | USA | Canada | Ireland | Australia
India | New Zealand | South Africa

Puffin Books is part of the Penguin Random House group of companies
whose addresses can be found at global.penguinrandomhouse.com.

www.penguin.co.uk www.puffin.co.uk www.ladybird.co.uk

First published in the USA by Scholastic Inc. and
in Great Britain by Puffin Books by arrangement with
Amulet Books, an imprint of ABRAMS, 2019

001



Book design by Jeff Kinney



Printed and bound in Great Britain by Clays Ltd, Elcograf S.p.A.

A CIP catalogue record for this book is available from the British Library

ISBN: 978-0-241-38882-2

All correspondence to:
Puffin Books
Penguin Random House Children's
80 Strand, London WC2R 0RL

Penguin Random House is committed to a
sustainable future for our business, our readers
and our planet. This book is made from Forest
Stewardship Council® certified paper.

The first thing you need to know about me is that I am Greg Heffley's best friend. I know it says that on the cover but I wanted to mention that in case you missed it.

You are probably wondering why I am writing a book about my best friend Greg Heffley.

Well the reason is because one day Greg is going to be rich and famous and he says everyone will want to know his whole life's story so they can make movies about him and stuff.

When I told Greg I thought that's what his DIARY was for he said it's not a diary it's a journal and he whapped me on the head with it.

Greg whaps me a LOT but in his defence sometimes I say stupid things.

Greg said his journal is his AUTObiography and he needs me to write his BIOGRAPHY.

He said there are probably gonna be a LOT of biographies about him and he was giving me the chance to write the first one. I figure nobody can do a better job than ME because like I said already, Greg is my best friend.

When I drew the cover I showed it to Greg and he said the title was dumb. Then he whapped me with it, but since it was only one page the whapping wasn't too bad.

Most biographies of famous people start with a chapter called "EARLY LIFE" or something like that so I am just gonna start this one the same way unless I can think of a better title in the next ten seconds.

## EARLY LIFE

To be honest with you I don't know a whole lot about Greg's early life because I only met him in the fourth grade. But here are some facts I DO know about him: Greg has a mom and a dad, just like I do.

But in case you are thinking me and Greg are basically the same person then you are wrong because Greg has two brothers and I am an only child.

Greg's older brother is Rodrick and he has a rock band called Löded Diper. Some of their songs have swears in them, so my mom and dad won't let me be at the Heffleys' house when Rodrick has band practice.

Greg's little brother is Manny and he is three. One time when I had a sleepover at Greg's, Manny just randomly pulled down his pants and showed me his bum.

Now every time I see Manny he acts like we have this big secret or something.

Greg's parents are just regular people so I can't really think of anything to say about them.

If this book was about ME then I would write a LOT about MY parents. My mom is awesome because she feeds me healthy food and helps me keep my body clean.

And my dad is my second best friend after Greg but don't tell my dad that.

Now that I brought up my dad I should probably mention that he is not such a big fan of Greg. And the reason I know that is because he is always saying it.

But I think the reason is because my dad doesn't get Greg's sense of humour.

Anyway that just about wraps up the chapter about Greg's early life. Hopefully Greg can give me some baby pictures or something to fill out this section because like I said before I don't have a whole lot of information until I get to the part where he's in the fourth grade.

## THE STUFF FROM FOURTH GRADE ON

I moved to Greg's street in the fourth grade so now this biography is gonna get a lot more detailed.

After me and Greg met we had a few playdates at MY house and a few playdates at HIS house. Oh yeah I forgot, Greg doesn't like it when I call them "playdates" so I will have to change that in my second draft or else I'm gonna get whapped again.

Anyway me and Greg "hung out" a lot at each other's houses but then one day he invited me to his house for a SLEEPOVER.

I was pretty nervous because I never stayed over at a friend's house before. In fact I wasn't even sleeping in my OWN bed yet because I was scared.

I told my mom I was too nervous to stay at Greg's but I got a little LESS nervous when she said I could take Carrots with me.

When I got to Greg's we hung out in his room for a while but at 9:00 Mrs Heffley said it was time to go to bed. And she said we had to sleep in the BASEMENT.

Well now I was SUPER nervous because I think basements are really creepy.

As soon as Mrs Heffley turned the lights off, Greg told me he needed to tell me something important. He said there's a half man, half goat that lives in the woods in our neighbourhood so I probably shouldn't go outside alone at night.

Well I was NOT happy to hear that news and I really wished someone told my parents about this goat guy before we moved into the neighbourhood.

Anyway the goat thing got me TOTALLY spooked so I hid under the covers. But I think Greg got pretty spooked too because he crawled under them WITH me.

Then all of a sudden there was this crazy noise right outside the window and it sounded exactly how a half man, half goat would sound.

Me and Greg didn't wanna get eaten by this goat guy so we got out of there as fast as we could.

But we almost died anyway because we trampled each other running up the stairs.

We locked ourselves in the laundry room so the goat man couldn't get us. But that's when we found out it wasn't the goat guy at ALL, it was just Greg's brother Rodrick playing a trick on us.

OK so this next part is embarrassing but since it's a biography I've gotta tell the whole truth: I wet my pants when we were in the basement and heard those noises outside.

Mrs Heffley gave me an extra pair of Greg's underwear but they didn't fit. So my dad had to come get me and bring me home, and it was a long time before I was allowed to go to Greg's for another sleepover.

## AN EVEN MORE SCARY STORY

OK while I'm on the topic of scary stuff I want to tell a story about something that happened a couple of years ago.

One time I was at my grandpa's log cabin with my dad for the weekend and we took a hike and I got kind of dirty. Well technically it was my DAD'S cabin because my grandpa died the year before.

I called my grandpa "Bampy", and the reason I called him that is because when I was two I couldn't say "Grampa".

But then even when I got older and I COULD say "Grampa" nobody would let me change it.

And when my grandpa got older it's the only word he really said.

So anyway back to the story. After I got dirty from that hike my dad said I had to take a shower. But Bampy's cabin is really old and it doesn't HAVE a shower, it just has one of those creepy old-fashioned tubs.

So after I filled up the tub with water and got in, here's what happened NEXT.

I heard footsteps coming down the hall and I thought it was my dad bringing me a towel or something.

Then the door opened real slow, but there was NO ONE THERE.

And if you're thinking "Oh Rowley it was probably your dad playing a trick on you," well guess what, it WASN'T.

My dad was getting some milk at the store and he didn't come back until like a half hour later.

I told my dad what happened with the door and he said it was probably just the "wind".

But I know what it was: the GHOST OF BAMPY.

## THE TIME I SAVED GREG FROM TEVIN LARKIN'S BIRTHDAY PARTY

OK I know that last chapter didn't have a lot of Greg in it but I wanted to mention that story real quick because the Bampy thing totally FREAKED ME OUT.

Greg is in this chapter but just to let you know I'm kind of the hero of this one.

There is a kid named Tevin Larkin who lives over on Speen Street and last summer his mom invited me and Greg to Tevin's birthday party. Me and Greg didn't wanna go because Tevin is hyper but both our moms said we HAD to.

It turned out that me and Greg were the ONLY kids invited to Tevin's party but we didn't know that until we got there.

After we gave Tevin his presents his mom said it was time for party activities.

The first activity was to watch this movie about a guy who could turn into a bear and an eagle and a bunch of other animals.

And when the movie was over, Tevin wanted to watch it AGAIN. But me and Greg told Tevin's mom we didn't wanna watch the movie a second time, so she said we could move on to the other activities like pin the tail on the donkey.

Well that just made Tevin MAD.

He got all wound up and started acting like the guy in the movie who could turn into animals.

I guess Tevin's mom was used to this sort of thing but me and Greg didn't know what we were supposed to do.

So we went out of the back door and waited in the backyard for Tevin to calm down.

But it didn't take long for Tevin to find us out there.

I guess Tevin had eaten ALL the cake so now he was acting TOTALLY nuts.

RARRRRR

I took a few steps back to get out of Tevin's way but that's when I fell into a ditch that was pretty deep.

Luckily the ditch wasn't TOO deep or I probably would've broken some bones. But when I started to climb out of the ditch I heard this buzzing noise all around me.

It turned out there was a HORNETS' NEST at the bottom of the ditch and they were all stirred up.

I got stung twelve times and my mom had to come pick me up early. And Greg hitched a ride with us so he got to go home early too.

Anyway Greg is always saying he "owes me" for getting him out of that party so that's why I thought it was important to put it in this book.

## THE TIME ME AND GREG DUG UP AN ANCIENT BURIAL GROUND

If you were spooked out by that Bampy story from before then you might want to skip this one.

OK if you are still reading, remember I warned you. One time me and Greg were playing Vikings and Ninjas in the woods and then some teenagers came by and ruined our fun.

BUT THAT'S NOT EVEN THE SCARY PART YET so keep reading.

Me and Greg went further back into the woods to get away from those teens. Greg said we should build a fort so if they came looking for us we could protect ourselves.

So we spent the rest of the afternoon making a fort out of sticks and logs.

Greg said we should put some rocks in our fort in case things got REALLY bad but it was starting to get dark and there weren't a lot of rocks lying around in the woods anyway.

But then I tripped over something and guess what? It was a big ROCK.

I told Greg I thought I sprained my ankle but he was a lot more interested in that rock than my injury.

Greg said it wasn't a rock, it was a GRAVESTONE and we'd just built our fort on an ANCIENT BURIAL GROUND.

I guess you already knew that was coming because it was in the title of this chapter. I'll probably change it later on so I don't give the surprise away.

Anyway me and Greg were TOTALLY spooked out by this ancient burial ground thing and by now it was REALLY dark out so we were extra scared.

Then all of a sudden Greg took off and left me behind. I don't really blame him because if I could've run I would've been out of there too.

When Greg got home it was his dinnertime and I think he kind of forgot I was out in the woods. Luckily my parents called Greg's house and that helped him remember about me.

So I guess the point of this chapter is that sometimes Greg forgets important stuff but I'm just gonna let that go because the rest of the time he's a great pal.

## GREG'S ACCOMPLISHMENTS

Every biography I've ever read for a school report has a chapter called "ACCOMPLISHMENTS" so I figure I'd better add that in here before I forget.

The problem is that Greg is only a kid and most of his accomplishments haven't happened yet. So I'll leave some blank space here and I can fill it in later on.

## THE TIME GREG PLAYED A HILARIOUS PRANK ON ME

Sometimes Greg can be pretty hilarious and that's what this chapter is about. This story has a twist ending and THIS time I'm not gonna give it away in the title.

One day me and Greg were hanging out at my house when my parents weren't home. Greg told me he saw on the news that there was a burglar going around breaking into people's houses.

Then he said he had to go home for dinner and once he left I started thinking about that burglar.

But here's the thing: I found out later that Greg just PRETENDED to leave. He shut the front door but then stayed in my house.

Then he took off his shoes and walked up the stairs super quiet so I couldn't hear him.

Then he started stomping around real loud upstairs. At first I thought it was the ghost of Bampy all over again.

Then I realized it was probably that burglar Greg mentioned and I almost peed my pants for the second time in this biography.

I heard footsteps coming down the stairs and I ran into the garage to hide from the burglar.

It was PITCH BLACK in the garage but I didn't want to make a move until I was sure that the burglar was gone.

Then all of a sudden the door to the garage opened real slow and I knew he was gonna get me if I didn't do something.

So I whacked him in the face with my dad's tennis racket and made a run for it.

Then I ran out of the front door and went to Mrs Monroe's house next door to tell her to call the cops.

But then Greg came out of my house and that's when I found out the whole thing was just one of his hilarious pranks.

Greg was mad at me for two whole weeks and said I should've known he is always joking around and that it was a prank.

I guess he's got a pretty good point about that since he is always playing wacky pranks on me. So I feel kind of bad about whacking him with a tennis racket.

but not really

## ANOTHER TIME GREG GOT MAD AT ME

OK there are actually a whole BUNCH of times that Greg got mad at me but this story happened on Tuesday so it's fresh in my mind.

Me and Greg were walking home from school and there were slugs everywhere because it just rained the night before. Whenever there are slugs lying around, Greg chases me with one.

I guess it's pretty funny if you think about it but it's never that funny when it's happening.

Luckily I am really fast when someone is chasing me with a slug so I got away from Greg by jumping up on the big rock in Mr Yee's front yard.

Greg tried to get me to climb down from the rock but I didn't really trust him.

Greg tried to fling the slug at me but he lost his balance and almost fell into a giant puddle in front of the rock. Greg was stuck and I felt bad for him because he is my best friend after all.

I got down from the rock and tried to help Greg. He told me to pull him back up to his feet but I guess I heard him wrong.

I grabbed him BY his feet and that turned out to be a pretty dumb move.

I spent the next three hours locked in my bedroom and I only came out after Greg got called home for dinner.

I'm still waiting for Greg to get me back for the puddle thing but he says he's gonna get revenge on me when I "least expect it". I just hope he hurries up and does something soon because I wanna get it over with.

## THE TIME ME AND GREG HAD A DOUBLE SLEEPOVER

OK you already know this from the title of the chapter, but this one time me and Greg had a TWO-NIGHT SLEEPOVER. And I'll bet you think we had a total blast and you want to read about all the wacky stuff we did but guess what, it was not that fun at ALL.

The reason this sleepover happened was because my Nana got sick and me and my parents were gonna go visit her but then Mrs Heffley said:

When my mom said yes, me and Greg were HYPED because we never had a two-night sleepover before. But I guess we should've waited until later to celebrate because of the whole Nana thing.

On Friday my mom packed my bag for the weekend and she put in an extra pair of underwear "just in case".

Plus she packed a picture of her and my dad so I could look at it if I missed them too much while they were gone.

Like I said before, the sleepover wasn't a lot of fun but it started off pretty good. We played video games in Greg's basement and ate snacks. Then we prank-called Scotty Douglas and he blew the whistle he keeps right by his phone for when we do that.

But then Mrs Douglas called Mrs Heffley to tell on us for prank-calling Scotty. Then Mrs Heffley told us we were "bullying" and that made me feel ashamed.

At 9:00 Mrs Heffley said it was time for bed and she went back upstairs.

I was pretty tired but Greg said he had an idea. There is this kid on our street named Joseph O'Rourke who has a trampoline but he never lets anyone use it. Greg said we should sneak out and jump on the trampoline while Joe was asleep.

Well I wasn't so crazy about this sneaking-out idea but Greg said if I was going to be a baby I should go up to Manny's room and sleep in THERE.

I said I wasn't a baby and he said "Yuh-huh" and I said "Nuh-uh." Then he said "Yuh-huh times INFINITY" but I was ready for that and I said "Nuh-uh times infinity SQUARED." And I thought I had Greg beat with that one, but he got me anyway when he said "Yuh-huh times infinity squared plus ONE."

So we snuck out of the back door and I followed Greg up to Joe's. It was really cold outside and all I had on were my jammies, but I didn't wanna complain because then Greg might call me a baby again.

Sure enough all the lights at the O'Rourkes' house were off so this was our big chance to use Joe's trampoline. Greg said we couldn't make any noise and then he climbed up and did a bunch of jumps but he was real quiet.

Then it was MY turn. This was my first time on a trampoline and it was REALLY fun and I guess that's why I forgot we were being sneaky.

The lights came on inside the O'Rourkes' house and their dog started barking and Greg took off without me. I wanted to run TOO but it's not so easy to stop bouncing when you're on a trampoline.

Once I finally stopped I ran to the Heffleys' house and went around to the back door.

But I guess Greg wanted to teach me a lesson for making too much noise at the O'Rourkes' because he wouldn't let me in.

I tried to show Greg that I was freezing but I don't think he really got what I was trying to tell him.

I thought he was gonna make me stay out there all NIGHT so I ran around the house to see if the front door was unlocked.

But it WASN'T and I kind of freaked out a little.

The good news is that someone came to the door pretty quick but the bad news is that it was Mr Heffley.

Mr Heffley told us to get our stuff from the basement because we were gonna have to stay in Greg's room so he could keep an eye on us.

Then Mrs Heffley came into Greg's room and said she was disappointed in us for sneaking out and that made me feel ashamed all over again. But I think Greg gets in trouble a LOT so he didn't seem that ashamed.

As soon as Mrs Heffley went to bed, Greg said I was dumb for making all that noise at the O'Rourkes' and EXTRA dumb for ringing the doorbell. I said I was sorry for saying "wheeee" on the trampoline but the doorbell thing was all his fault.

Then Greg whapped me with his pillow and I whapped him BACK but I guess we made too much noise and that's why I had to see Mr Heffley in his underwear for the second time in one night.

Mr Heffley told Greg he had to sleep in Manny's room and all I could think was, who's the baby NOW?

The next day Mrs Heffley woke me up and said breakfast was ready downstairs.

Greg was in the bathroom brushing his teeth and he said he hoped I brought my own toothpaste because if I wanted to use his I was gonna have to pay for it since it was his house.

I told him I DID have my own toothpaste and then he said I was gonna have to pay for the water I used to brush my teeth.

I said I wasn't gonna pay for the water because I was the guest and guests are supposed to get treated SPECIAL.

So he said if I wasn't gonna pay what I owed I couldn't eat breakfast or any other meals either.

I was like yeah RIGHT and then he said I was using his electricity and he shut the light off on me.

When I got downstairs I told Mrs Heffley about all the stuff Greg said upstairs and she said I was RIGHT about guests being special.

Then she let me pick which pancakes I wanted before Greg got to pick.

After breakfast Mrs Heffley said we had too much screen time the day before and that we had to figure out something to do until lunch.

Greg was in a grumpy mood so I decided to cheer him up with a knock-knock joke. But he wouldn't do the "who's there" part no matter how many times I tried.

I told Greg I was gonna go upstairs and tell his mom he wasn't saying "who's there". And that finally made him do it.

So then I said, what do elephants do at night? But Greg said you're not supposed to ask a question in that part of a knock-knock joke and I said yes you are.

Then he told me I was dumb and I said I was gonna tell on him for THAT. And Greg said go right ahead and so I DID.

So Mrs Heffley came down and told Greg he wasn't allowed to call me dumb or stupid or any other bad names either.

But then when she left Greg said he had a new nickname for me. At first I thought it sounded cool but then I figured out what he MEANT.

I told Greg I was gonna tell on him AGAIN but then Greg said that it was Opposite Day and everything meant the opposite of what it was supposed to.

Well I knew what he MEANT so I went and told Mrs Heffley. But at first she didn't get mad because she didn't know it was Opposite Day.

So then I explained it to Mrs Heffley and she made Greg apologize. But I think he might've been being opposite.

Mrs Heffley told us that sometimes friends get on each other's nerves but we needed to figure things out since we had a whole day to go on our sleepover.

She said maybe we should spend some time apart and I thought that sounded like a GREAT idea. So I hung out with Manny in his room for a while.

Even though I was having fun with Manny, I missed my mom and dad and I looked at their picture whenever I got the chance.

The next time I saw Greg was when we had lunch. Mrs Heffley made peanut butter and jelly sandwiches and she even remembered to cut the crusts off mine.

After we finished our sandwiches she gave us chocolate chip-cookies as dessert. She gave Greg one but she gave me TWO because she said I was the guest and guests are SPECIAL.

I ate one of my cookies but I made a shield around the other cookie with my arms so Greg couldn't get it. Sometimes if I have something Greg wants he will lick it so I won't want it any more.

That's what he did last Halloween when I got more candy than he did.

But Greg said he was full and didn't even WANT my cookie. He said that while I was playing with Manny he was reading a book about magic and he wanted to show me a trick. I really like magic so I said OK.

First Greg told me to put my fingers on the edge of the table so they were close together like this:

Then Greg took my glass of milk and put it on top of my fingers.

I asked him when the magic part was gonna happen and he said it was ALREADY happening because I couldn't move. Well he was right because if I did, the glass of milk would tip over and spill. And Mr Heffley gets mad when I spill stuff in his house.

But then Greg said here's the REAL magic part and he took my cookie and ate it up.

After that, Greg went upstairs but I was stuck at the kitchen table. And I was still there a half hour later when Mrs Heffley came back to the kitchen.

I told her what Greg did and boy was she mad but it wasn't because of the magic trick. She was mad that Greg took something that belonged to me without asking.

We went up to Greg's room and Mrs Heffley told me I could pick out one of Greg's things to take home with me so we'd be even.

Well Greg had a BUNCH of cool toys that he never lets me play with so it was really hard to pick. But every time I got close to one of his favourites he kind of let me know I shouldn't pick that one.

So I picked an action figure that was a knight with a missing arm and Greg seemed OK with that.

But as soon as Mrs Heffley left the room Greg said I could play with my lame action figure because he was gonna play with all his cool stuff by himself.

It kind of bugged me and I wanted to bug Greg BACK. So I pretended I was having a total blast with my toy.

Well it WORKED and Greg said he wanted his action figure BACK. I said no way and he said he was just gonna wait for me to fall asleep and he'd take it back HIMSELF.

I told him I was gonna put the action figure down my underwear so he couldn't get it and he didn't like that idea.

Then Greg said he'd TRADE me for the action figure and I asked him what he'd give me for it. Greg said he'd give me ninety-nine cents for the knight and I said OK to that.

But then Greg took off his sock and tried to get me to smell it.

And I was like, what was that for? And Greg said that was my first "scent".

I said I wanted ninety-nine CENTS not ninety-nine SCENTS. But Greg said a deal's a deal and then he tried to get me to smell his other sock as part two of my payment.

When I told Greg I was gonna go tell on him again, Greg said he'd trade me his Lego dragon for my knight and I said YES because that dragon is way better than a knight with no arm.

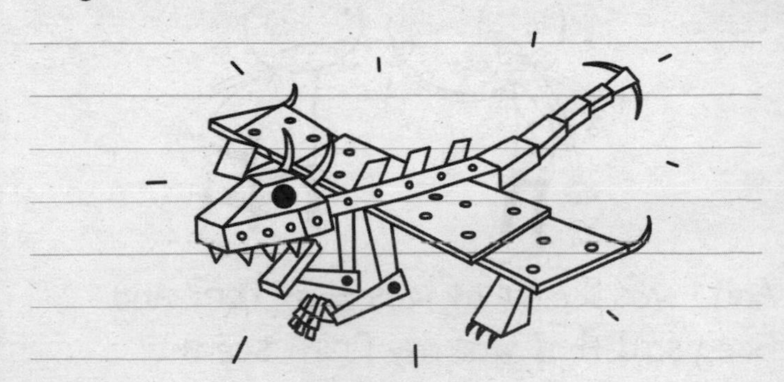

But then when I gave Greg my knight he wouldn't give me the dragon because he said I should've remembered it was still Opposite Day.

Well that was the last straw for me and I tried to grab the dragon from Greg. But I kind of forgot it was made of Lego and it broke apart.

I guess we were making a lot of noise because the next thing we knew Mrs Heffley was back in Greg's room. She said she was gonna have to separate us for the rest of the night which was fine with ME.

Mrs Heffley said that we each had one half of the bedroom and that we had to stay on our own side. So she asked me which side I wanted and I picked the side with the BED which made Greg mad.

When Mrs Heffley went back to her room, Greg said he was turning on an invisible force field between our two sides.

Then he said if someone crossed over they'd get zapped.

Greg said he was fine with me having the bed because he could sleep on an air mattress and plus all the fun stuff was on HIS side of the room. And when I reached over to Greg's side for my action figure sure enough I got zapped.

I opened the drawer in the table next to Greg's bed to see if he had any comics I could read. Well there weren't any comics but one of Greg's old handheld video games was in there.

So I played it and Greg couldn't do anything because of the force field.

But Greg said I could play video games by myself like a nerd because he was having a wild party on HIS side of the room and I wasn't invited. And I got kind of jealous because his party looked pretty fun.

So I said well I'm having a party on MY side and it was even more wild than HIS party and I had really good music. Greg said I was lame because I couldn't even come up with an original idea but I still think he was kind of jealous of my party.

Then Greg said the plug to my party speakers was on HIS side of the room so he pulled it out to shut off my music.

Greg got back to his party and I tried to tell him to plug my speakers back in but Greg couldn't hear me because the music at his party was too loud.

But this time MR Heffley came into the room and he looked like he must've been asleep.

Mr Heffley said he didn't want one more peep out of us and then he left the room. We were both quiet for a long time but then Greg tried to get me to laugh and I almost did.

I was kind of glad we had to be quiet because I was getting pretty sleepy anyway and I wanted to go to bed.

I told Greg I needed to brush my teeth and he said too bad because the force field was still on and I was trapped in my half of the room for the whole night.

So I asked if he could just turn off the force field for a little while to brush my teeth but he said once the force field is turned on it stays on until the morning.

And then Greg went to the bathroom to brush HIS teeth and came back to the room after he was done.

That's when I remembered I need to use the bathroom before I go to bed every night so I don't have any accidents.

But Greg said I was just gonna have to hold it until the morning. I said I couldn't MAKE it all the way to morning and Greg said that wasn't his problem.

So I said if Greg didn't shut off the force field I was gonna have to pee into the Chewbacca mug on the table next to Greg's bed. Then he told me he had a special invisible knife that could cut through the force field.

Greg showed me how the knife worked by cutting a square in the force field right next to the table where the mug was.

Then he reached through the hole and grabbed the mug before I could stop him.

I told Greg that he could cut a BIG hole in the force field so I could get through it to use the bathroom.

But Greg said the knife ran on invisible batteries and they got used up when he made HIS hole so I was out of luck.

Then Greg started talking about all sorts of things that made me feel like I needed to go to the bathroom even MORE.

Finally Greg got tired and he fell asleep. I thought about trying to sneak past him but I was worried he was just faking it and I was gonna get zapped.

After a while I fell asleep too. But I woke up around six in the morning feeling like I was gonna BURST.

I didn't care about the force field any more but I was worried that if I used the bathroom I might wake up Mr Heffley. But I should've just used the bathroom anyway because Mr Heffley was already up for the day.

Luckily Mr Heffley didn't look up in time to see me at the window and when he got up to Greg's room I was already back in bed.

I fell back asleep after a while and got up when Mrs Heffley said it was time for breakfast. After we ate, Manny wanted to play with me and I went to get my knight action figure from Greg's room. But I couldn't find it ANYWHERE.

Greg said he didn't know what happened to it, but Mrs Heffley said he had to help me look for it.

So the two of us searched Greg's room but to be honest Greg wasn't being that helpful.

I guess Mrs Heffley thought Greg was hiding the action figure from me because she said if he didn't hand it over in two minutes then he was gonna be in big trouble.

Greg said he'd keep looking after he went to the bathroom but he was acting all suspicious and I'm pretty sure he had something in his hand.

Greg locked the bathroom door and Mrs Heffley told him to come out right this instant. But then the toilet flushed and when Greg opened the door there wasn't anything in his hand any more.

So Mrs Heffley made Greg give me THREE toys and this time I picked out ones that WEREN'T broken.

My mom and dad came and got me just before lunch and boy was I glad to see them. And P.S. if you wanted to know the answer to that knock-knock joke, it's "elephants watch elevision".

## THE TIME ME AND GREG DID SOME COMICS AND I HAD TO ___ THE CHEESE

This one is kind of a long story but I'll give you the short version.

In our first year of middle school me and Greg worked on a comic together called "Zoo-Wee Mama" and then Greg got bored of it and said I should do it by myself.

And then my comic got in the school paper and Greg was mad at me even though he's the one who TOLD me I should do it. And then a bunch of teenagers made me eat a piece of ________ that was on the basketball court.

I still can't eat pizza or mozzarella sticks or anything else with _ _ _ _ _ _ _ _ in it but Greg says I need to "get over it" because that happened a long time ago.

But that's not what this chapter is about. I just found some Zoo-Wee Mama comics me and Greg did that never got in the school newspaper.

I asked Greg what I should do with them and he said I should hold on to them for when he gets famous.

I figured I'd lose them again so I put them in this book just in case.

That mad scientist has been chasing us for days and I am starving!
A giant strawberry! We are saved!
Oh no we got shrunk down to the size of bugs!
ZOO-WEE MAMA!
I have been working on this Eiffel Tower model for ten whole years!
Time to bring it out of the basement and show it to the world!
Oh no it doesn't fit through the doorway!
CRUNCH
ZOO-WEE MAMA!
Merry Christmas Balg.
You dummy it's 12,000 B.C. and Christmas hasn't even been invented yet.
ZOO-WEE MAMA!

## THE ADVENTURES OF GREG AND ROWLEY

I'm pretty much up to date on Greg's life so today I showed Greg what I wrote so far. I thought he would like it but he was MAD.

Greg said this book was supposed to be about HIM and not about ME. I told him it was hard to write about just HIM because most of the time we do stuff TOGETHER.

He said I need to go back through the book and take out all the stuff with me in it. I told him that would be dumb because then the book would only be like one page long.

I said maybe we should change the title to "THE ADVENTURES OF GREG AND ROWLEY" and it could be OUR biography.

Then I said since there's a lot of scary stuff in this book we could make it into a spooky series where these two pals solve mysteries. We could make a lot of money and we'd BOTH be rich and famous.

Greg said that was the stupidest idea he ever heard.

He said this book is about HIS life and if he wants to he can just change the name of Greg's best friend to "Rupert" and then he wouldn't owe me ANYTHING. Plus he said he'd make Rupert really dumb and drooling all the time.

Then Greg told me the book smelled funny anyway and when I brought it up to my nose to sniff it he shut the book in my face real hard.

So I said, hey what was THAT for? and Greg said that's what I got for dropping him in the puddle. Then he said he got me back when I least expected it and I guess he was right about THAT.

But I was pretty mad anyway and I whapped him with the book which is pretty heavy now that it's got all these pages in it.

Well I guess Greg wasn't expecting THAT because he lost his balance and fell into a big puddle.

Anyway I am up in my room now and I am hoping Greg's mom calls him home for bedtime soon because he already skipped dinner.

I'm glad all that stuff happened today because it gave me a whole new chapter in our biography. I'm sure we'll be pals again tomorrow and we'll have a bunch of new adventures that I can put in here.

And I'll bet if we go with my idea about the scary stuff it'll sell a million copies.

But if Greg changes my name to Rupert I just want to say for the record that he wet his pants at that first sleepover too.

# Love Diary of a Wimpy Kid?

**Read on for a sneak preview of a BRAND-NEW and HILARIOUS story from Puffin Books.**

# CHAPTER 1

This is Charles McGuffin.

It isn't *actually* him. It's just a picture of him. OF COURSE. If you hadn't figured that out, this book will be way too difficult for you and you should probably go and read *The Really Simple Book of Dead Easy Stories for Total Numptyheads* instead.

Charles McGuffin was just like you and me. Well, he wasn't like me because I'm big and hairy, and Charles is small and pretty smooth. So he's just like you. Except he has a you-know-what, and I'm guessing many of you reading this don't have a you-know-what. So Charles is like *some* of you.

Except for one **MAJORLY HUGE, MASSIVE** difference.

He can change into animals.

As in, one minute he's a normal boy, the next minute he's a wolf.

Or an armadillo.

Or a danger noodle (which, as everyone knows, is the actual scientific name for a snake).

OK, so that probably means Charles is absolutely *nothing* like any of you because nobody else can change into animals.

I think it's probably best if we start this book again, don't you?

Just pretend you didn't read this bit, OK?

# CHAPTER 1 (AGAIN)

This is Charles McGuffin.

It isn't *actually* him. It's just a picture of him. **OF COURSE.**

Charles McGuffin is absolutely nothing like you or me. He is totally, completely different. Charles is *unique*. Because Charles can transform into animals. Like danger noodles.

Now, Charlie[1] was a pretty normal boy until about three weeks after his ninth birthday. He'd just come back from visiting his older brother, SmoothMove, at the hospital for the zillionth time. SmoothMove was quite ill and had been in hospital for ages and ages. This was really annoying because Charlie was convinced he could now beat his brother at *FIFA* on the PS4 and wanted to prove it. Also, the den in the garden needed mending and Charlie couldn't do

[1] Although he's called Charles, everybody calls him Charlie for short, which is pretty silly because Charlie actually has the same number of letters as Charles.

P.S. This is called a footnote. It's called a footnote because when a clever person from ancient Greece thought of something really important and absolutely had to write it down so they didn't forget it, but didn't have any paper to write it on, they used to write it on their foot.

You know what, I'm not too sure about that fact. Don't trust me on that one.

Get Well
SOON

it by himself. And sometimes Charlie just wanted his brother back so he had someone to play hide-and-seek with. Playing hide-and-seek by yourself isn't much fun – Charlie had tried.

If you're very clever, you might have guessed that Charlie's brother isn't *actually* called SmoothMove, but woe betide[2] you if you were to call him anything else. Charlie's brother's actual name was Henry, but after a lifetime of being called Horrid Henry he would punch anybody right on the nose if they called him by his real name. He was twelve years old, sick of hospital and could still easily beat Charlie at *FIFA*, no matter what Charlie said. And he might have a girlfriend, but he would punch you on the nose if you said, 'SmoothMove has a girlfriend.' In fact, you'd do well to come away

[2] Well spotted! It's another footnote. You're probably wondering what 'woe betide' means. Well, only parents and teachers are allowed to say, 'Woe betide you . . .' It's the law. But, if you want some fun, next time a teacher or parent says, 'Woe betide you,' ask them what it means. What it means *exactly*. You will probably see steam coming out of their ears and you'll get into more trouble but it will be worth it.

from any conversation with Charlie's brother without getting punched on the nose for one reason or another.

As soon as Charlie and his mum and dad got home from visiting SmoothMove, Charlie ran straight upstairs to his bedroom. He dived into his bed, under his duvet, and tried not to think about the **'big scan'** that his brother had just been telling him about. After a while, he wiped his eyes and propped the duvet up with a tennis racquet to turn his bed into a tent. Once the tent was steady and stopped collapsing, he switched on his torch and began reading his favourite book. Charlie's favourite book was about volcanoes. It had pictures of massive explosions and orangey-red lava, and he liked to imagine he was escaping certain death by sliding down the volcano, surfing lava and dodging explosions.

The sound of his parents arguing downstairs

rumbled through the house, low like thunder. Charlie closed his book. He couldn't concentrate. Darkness had fallen outside, and the street light outside Charlie's window was making uncanny shadows on his bedroom wall. The silhouettes of the tree branches looked a little too much like long, clutching witches' fingers for Charlie's liking, so, quick as a flash, he sprang out of bed and pulled his curtains together.

It was there and then that it first happened.

It began with a twitching in his eye. Charlie froze to the spot, feeling his eyelid blink manically. His eye had twitched before, when he'd been tired, but this felt different somehow. It felt like somebody had just plugged him into a wall socket. The twitching spread to his other eye, and both eyes were blinking and twitching.

A feeling burst through the whole of his body, like he'd just been shot through an electrical wire, like *he* was the electricity. Every part of his body **FIZZED** and **HUMMED**. The fizzing and humming became stronger, until he felt he was on fire, but a fire inside a never-ending tube, squeezed and vibrating.

His skin felt extraordinary. Alive. He looked at his arm and, with some considerable alarm, saw that hair was sprouting out of every part of his skin.

Weirdly the room was growing larger too.

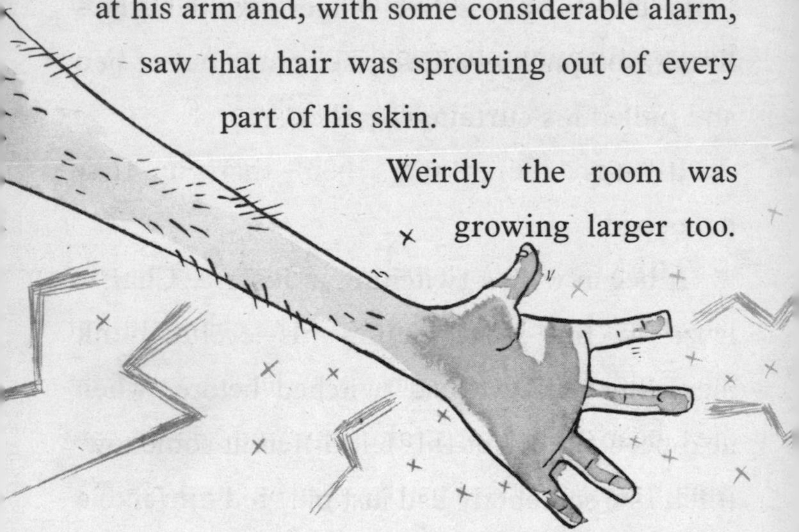

But no, Charlie realized, the room wasn't growing larger – it was him who was shrinking! Smaller and smaller he shrank, the room growing ever larger around him.

And his body – Charlie hardly dared look – his body was transforming. Completely. Extra legs were growing out of him (which is every bit as gross as you could imagine). And finally he felt new eyes emerging out of his head (which was possibly even grosser than the new legs).

Charlie recognized almost immediately that he was turning into a spider.

And how did Charlie know this?

He looked at the *evidence*:

**EVIDENCE 1:** Charlie was now tiny. Admittedly he hadn't been that huge before he changed, but he could see a dried apricot under his bed that he'd been saving for a rainy day, and he was now about the same size as the apricot. And normal nine-year-old boys usually aren't the size of dried apricots.

**EVIDENCE 2:** Charlie counted his legs and he

had eight of them, which is about six too many legs for a human, but just the right number for a spider.

**EVIDENCE 3:** He was completely covered in short brown hair. Now, being covered in hair didn't necessarily stop someone from being human – take Charlie's Uncle Pete, for instance. Uncle Pete had taken Charlie swimming once and

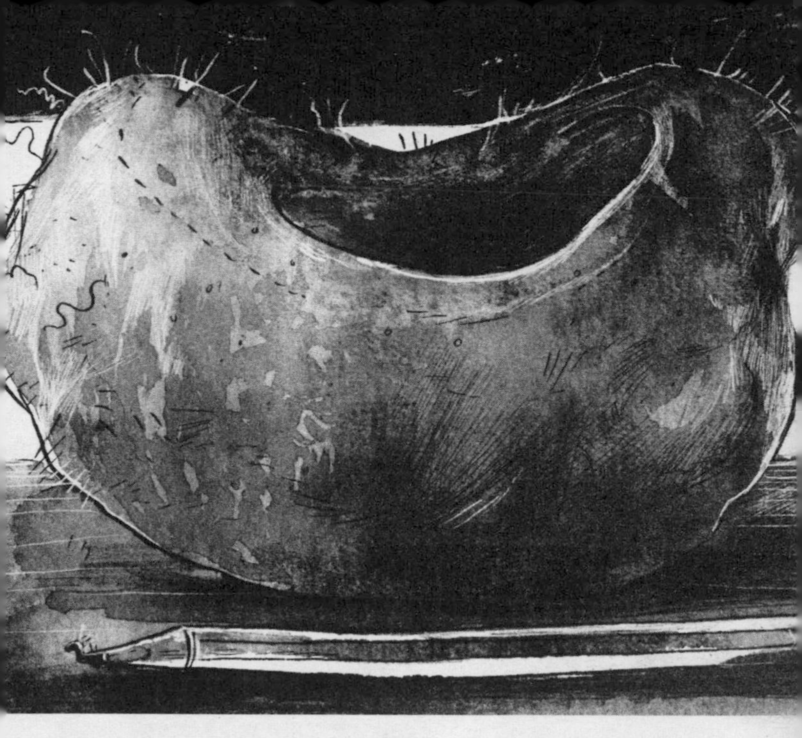

when he took off his T-shirt he had a back so covered in thick tufty hair a gorilla would have been jealous. All the other children had stopped and stared, wide-eyed and jaws agape, as Uncle Pete stepped into the pool, back hair fluttering in the breeze. Charlie had tried to forget this ever happened but the more he tried to forget Uncle Pete's Hairy Back, the more it stayed in his brain because brains are annoying like that.

SPONSORED BY

SHARE A STORY

Well **hello** there! We are

Overjoyed that you have **joined our celebration** of

Reading **books** and **sharing stories**, because we

Love bringing **books** to you.

Did you know, we are a **charity** dedicated to celebrating the

Brilliance of **reading for pleasure** for everyone, everywhere?

Our mission is to help you discover **brand new stories** and

Open your mind to exciting **new worlds** and **characters**, from

**Kings** and **queens** to **wizards** and **pirates** to **animals** and **adventurers** and so many more. We couldn't

Do it without all the amazing **authors** and **illustrators**, **booksellers** and **bookshops**, **publishers**, **schools** and **libraries** out there –

And most importantly, we couldn't do it all without . . .

YOU!

**On your bookmarks, get set, READ!**
**Happy Reading. Happy World Book Day.**